Let's Discover Canada

SASKATCHEWAN

by
Suzanne LeVert

George Sheppard
McMaster University
General Editor

CHELSEA HOUSE PUBLISHERS
New York   Philadelphia

Cover: A farm with a tall grain elevator on Saskatchewan's green prairie.
Opposite: Dancers perform at Vesna, the Ukrainian festival of spring, in Saskatoon.

Chelsea House Publishers
EDITOR-IN-CHIEF: Remmel Nunn
MANAGING EDITOR: Karyn Gullen Browne
COPY CHIEF: Juliann Barbato
PICTURE EDITOR: Adrian G. Allen
ART DIRECTOR: Maria Epes
DEPUTY COPY CHIEF: Mark Rifkin
ASSISTANT ART DIRECTOR: Noreen Romano
MANUFACTURING MANAGER: Gerald Levine
SYSTEMS MANAGER: Lindsey Ottman
PRODUCTION MANAGER: Joseph Romano
PRODUCTION COORDINATOR: Marie Claire Cebrián

Let's Discover Canada
SENIOR EDITOR: Rebecca Stefoff

Staff for SASKATCHEWAN
COPY EDITOR: Brian Sookram
EDITORIAL ASSISTANT: Ian Wilker
PICTURE RESEARCHER: Sandy Jones
DESIGNER: Diana Blume

Library of Congress Cataloging-in-Publication Data

LeVert, Suzanne.
    Let's discover Canada. Saskatchewan/by Suzanne LeVert: George Sheppard, general editor.
       p. cm.
    Includes bibliographical references and index.
    Summary: Discusses the history, geography, and culture of the
Canadian province of Saskatchewan.
    ISBN 0-7910-1024-4
    1. Saskatchewan—Juvenile literature. [1. Saskatchewan.] I. Sheppard, George C. B.
    II. Title.   90-46036
F1071.L48   1991   CIP
971.24—dc20   AC

Contents

"My Canada" by Pierre Berton   4
Saskatchewan at a Glance   7
The Land   9
The History   19
The Economy   37
The People   43
The Cities   49
Things to Do and See   55
Festivals   58
Chronology   60
Further Reading   61
Index   62

My Canada

by Pierre Berton

"Nobody knows my country," a great Canadian journalist, Bruce Hutchison, wrote almost half a century ago. It is still true. Most Americans, I think, see Canada as a pleasant vacationland and not much more. And yet we are the United States's greatest single commercial customer, and the United States is our largest customer.

Lacking a major movie industry, we have made no wide-screen epics to chronicle our triumphs and our tragedies. But then there has been little blood in our colonial past—no revolutions, no civil war, not even a wild west. Yet our history is crammed with remarkable men and women. I am thinking of Joshua Slocum, the first man to sail alone around the world, and Robert Henderson, the prospector who helped start the Klondike gold rush. I am thinking of some of our famous artists and writers—comedian Dan Aykroyd, novelists Margaret Atwood and Robertson Davies, such popular performers as Michael J. Fox, Anne Murray, Gordon Lightfoot, and k.d. lang, and hockey greats from Maurice Richard to Gordie Howe to Wayne Gretzky.

The real shape of Canada explains why our greatest epic has been the building of the Pacific Railway to unite the nation from

sea to sea in 1885. On the map, the country looks square. But because the overwhelming majority of Canadians live within 100 miles (160 kilometers) of the U.S. border, in practical terms the nation is long and skinny. We are in fact an archipelago of population islands separated by implacable barriers—the angry ocean, three mountain walls, and the Canadian Shield, that vast desert of billion-year-old rock that sprawls over half the country, rich in mineral treasures, impossible for agriculture.

Canada's geography makes the country difficult to govern and explains our obsession with transportation and communication. The government has to be as involved in railways, airlines, and broadcasting networks as it is with social services such as universal medical care. Rugged individualism is not a Canadian quality. Given the environment, people long ago learned to work together for security.

It is ironic that the very bulwarks that separate us—the chiseled peaks of the Selkirk Mountains, the gnarled scarps north of Lake Superior, the ice-choked waters of the Northumberland Strait —should also be among our greatest attractions for tourists and artists. But if that is the paradox of Canada, it is also the glory.

Saskatchewan's wide open spaces and rolling grasslands beckoned settlers from Europe and eastern North America as Canada's frontier was pushed westward.

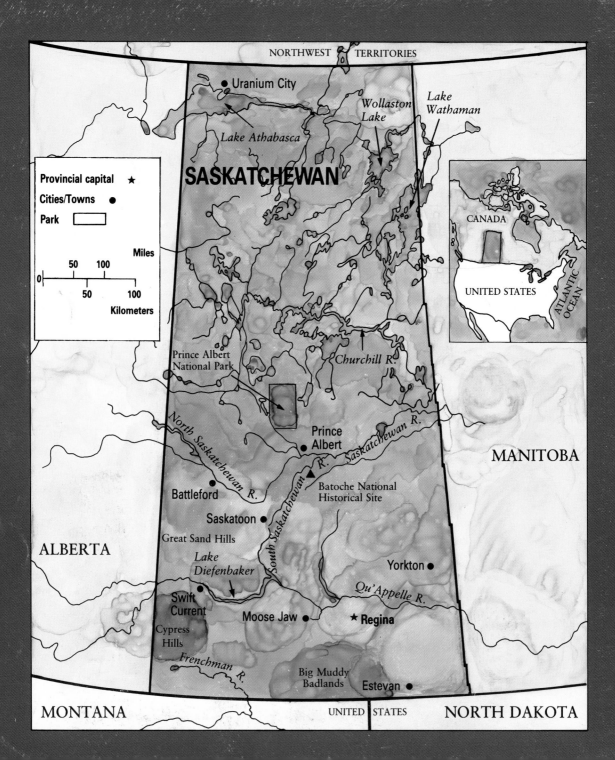

NORTHWEST TERRITORIES

• Uranium City

Lake Athabasca

SASKATCHEWAN

Wollaston Lake

Lake Wathaman

Provincial capital ★
Cities/Towns ●
Park ▭

Miles
50 100
0
50 100
Kilometers

CANADA

UNITED STATES

ATLANTIC OCEAN

Churchill R.

Prince Albert
National Park

North Saskatchewan R.

Prince
Albert

Saskatchewan R.

MANITOBA

▲ Batoche National
Historical Site

Battleford ●

South Saskatchewan R.

Saskatoon ●

Great Sand Hills

Lake Diefenbaker

Yorkton ●

ALBERTA

Qu'Appelle R.

Swift
Current ●

Cypress
Hills

Moose Jaw ●   ★ **Regina**

Frenchman R.

Big Muddy
Badlands   Estevan ●

MONTANA

UNITED STATES

NORTH DAKOTA

Western red lily

Sharp-tailed grouse

Saskatchewan at a Glance

Capital: Regina

Largest cities: Regina, Saskatoon, Moose Jaw

Population: 1,009,000 (1986 census)

Languages: 92.8 percent English, 1 percent French, 6.2 percent other

Entered Canadian confederation: September 1, 1905

Area: 251,700 square miles (651,900 square kilometers)

Elevation: Highest point in Cypress Hills, 4,546 feet (1,386 meters); lowest point at Lake Athabasca shore, 699 feet (213 meters)

Provincial flower: Western red lily (also known as prairie lily)

Provincial flag: Equal horizontal bars of green above, yellow below, with a prairie lily in the left half and the coat of arms in the upper right

Coat of arms: Three sheaves of wheat on a green background in lower part to represent the province's leading position in wheat production, a red lion on a yellow background across the top to represent loyalty to the Crown

Provincial bird: Sharp-tailed grouse

Government: Parliamentary system with a single-chamber legislative assembly of 64 members, popularly elected by district for terms of 5 years; the province's lieutenant governor is its formal head of government, appointed by federal government as representative of the Crown; the province's premier and the members of the executive council are members of the legislative assembly; 6 appointed senators and 14 elected members of the legislature represent Saskatchewan in federal government in Ottawa

The Land

Known as Canada's Breadbasket, Saskatchewan is one of the largest wheat producers in the world. In fact, more than two-fifths of Canada's farmland lies in this agriculturally rich province, and Saskatchewan's farmers produce almost 60 percent of Canada's wheat.

Covering approximately 251,700 square miles (651,900 square kilometers), Saskatchewan is the only one of Canada's provinces that has no natural boundaries such as rivers or sea-coasts. It is one of only two provinces that do not have saltwater coastlines (the other is Alberta). Saskatchewan is bordered by the United States to the south, the Northwest Territories to the north, the province of Manitoba to the east, and the province of Alberta to the west. At its longest and widest, this rectangular province spans 760 miles (1,225 kilometers) from north to south and 395 miles (630 kilometers) from east to west.

Although Saskatchewan is often associated only with prairies and grain, its terrain is far from flat and monotonous. There are many startling geographic contrasts within the province, which has three distinct types of terrain from north to south.

Opposite: farms and wheat fields that stretch across the province in a belt of fertile prairie make Saskatchewan Canada's Breadbasket.
Above: the wilderness has been preserved in Prince Albert National Park. Here a moose cow and her calf feast on summer's lush vegetation.

Nearly 70 million barrels of crude petroleum are pumped from Saskatchewan's oil fields each year—more than 10 percent of Canada's total oil production.

The northern third of Saskatchewan is part of the forest and lake landscape that is found across most of the Canadian Shield, a vast, horseshoe-shaped geologic formation that covers almost half of Canada and dips into the United States. The Canadian Shield took on its present form during the last Ice Age, which began about 1.8 million years ago. At that time, most of the shield's soil was scraped away by glaciers, wind, and water, leaving much of this large region rocky and infertile. The retreat of the glaciers also created Saskatchewan's deepest lakes and rivers. Today, the northernmost part of the province is a watery place, with hundreds of lakes and streams as well as a great deal of muskeg (a type of wet, mossy swamp). Although large-scale farming is impossible in the thin and inhospitable soil, forests of aspen, jack pine, and spruce are found there. A bit more than half of the province—some 135,000 square miles (350,000 square kilometers)—is forested, and about 45,000 square miles (114,000 square kilometers) of timber is available for logging. Most of the forests suitable for logging lie north of the city of Prince Albert, in an irregular belt about 150 miles (240 kilometers) wide. Within these abundant forests live great herds of elk, moose, and caribou. Fur-bearing animals such as beavers, mink, otters, and bears also make their home in the northern woods.

In addition to its varied wildlife, northern Saskatchewan contains valuable minerals, including uranium, gold, copper, and zinc. The mining of these resources, especially uranium, has contributed greatly to the growth of Saskatchewan's economy in recent decades.

Central Saskatchewan—the grain belt—also owes its unique characteristics to the Ice Age. As the last glaciers retreated, rivers carried soil away from the rock exposed by the glaciers and into large lakes that formed in low-lying places. These lakes later drained away, leaving behind the thick layer of fertile soil that covers about a third of Saskatchewan, making it one of the most agriculturally productive areas in North America. The dark brown or black soil consists of heavy clay that can hold twice as

The rugged terrain of the Cypress Hills region in the southwest includes the province's highest point, which is 4,546 feet (1,386 meters) above sea level.

Grasslands National Park, along the valley of the Frenchman River, was the first park in North America set aside to preserve a section of the original short-grass prairie that once covered much of the continent's heart. Prairie dogs, sage grouse, and antelope live in these grasslands.

much water as can the soil that covers much of eastern Canada—an important consideration in Saskatchewan's rather dry climate. This clay also absorbs many vital nutrients and minerals needed for plant growth.

Central Saskatchewan has more than fertile soil to offer, however. Major oil fields were discovered there in the 1950s and now contribute significantly to the provincial economy. Vast reserves of potash, a compound that is important in the manufacture of fertilizer, have also been discovered in this region. In addition to their economic importance, the prairies of Saskatchewan are also quite beautiful. Far from being totally flat, they are dotted with hills in many areas, and when the wind blows through the wheat fields the landscape appears to be covered with smooth, rolling waves.

South of the grain belt is the third of Saskatchewan's distinct geographic areas, a region of many hills and valleys. The Cypress Hills region in the southwestern corner of the province contains the highest elevations in Canada between the Rocky Mountains in the west and Labrador in the east. These hills are called Mun-a-tuk-gaw, or "beautiful highlands," by the Indians. A large provincial park here contains some of the most varied plant and animal life in the province. Just north of Cypress Hills is a large patch of dunes called the Great Sand Hills. Another geologic wonder in southern Saskatchewan is the Big Muddy Badlands, a stretch of dusty land with no vegetation at all, where the stark landscape is marked by sandstone buttes and sharp cliffs.

Waterways

About 12 percent of Saskatchewan is covered by fresh water, most of it in the north. The province's streams and rivers form parts of four major drainage basins: the Mackenzie and the Churchill in the north and the Saskatchewan and the Qu'Appelle-Assiniboine in the south. The mighty Churchill River is actually a system of lakes connected by often spectacular rapids. Many of these waterways eventually flow into Lake Athabasca, which is located in the far north near Uranium City. The largest lake in Saskatchewan, Lake Athabasca covers some 3,100 square miles (8,080 square kilometers), extending into Alberta in the west.

Southern Saskatchewan contains one of the region's most important waterways, the Saskatchewan River. This river played a crucial role in the initial exploration and later development of the province; in fact, the Cree Indian name for the river, Kisiskadjewan or Kis-is-ska-tche-wan, meaning "swift flowing," gave the province its name. The Saskatchewan River is formed by the union of the North and South Saskatchewan rivers. From its headwaters in Alberta to its mouth in Lake Winnipeg in Manitoba, the Saskatchewan River is approximately 1,200 miles (1,922 kilometers) long. The Saskatchewan and its branches are vital waterways.

This placid stretch of the Churchill River offers fine canoeing. Elsewhere the river roars over thundering falls and boils through rapids.

Sand dunes and dead trees line the southern shore of Lake Athabasca in the northwest corner of the province. The stark beauty of this remote district around Saskatchewan's biggest lake attracts hardy vacationers, who explore the area from Uranium City, a mining center north of the lake.

Water has been tremendously important in the story of Saskatchewan. Not only did the rivers provide transportation for the early settlers, but modern Saskatchewan's economy requires a steady and plentiful water supply. Both agriculture and industry, particularly the production of potash, consume large quantities of water. Unfortunately, the amount of water available in the southern half of the province is highly unpredictable. The river systems in the agricultural regions carry water that comes mainly from the snowmelt in the Rocky Mountains, far to the west of Saskatchewan. Mild winters in the Rockies, then, can cause hardship for the farmer in Saskatchewan. Lake Diefenbaker on the

Dogsledding, once the only way to travel during the long, bitter winters, is now part of winter festivals such as this one in Regina.

South Saskatchewan River was created in 1958 as a reservoir, and some attempts have been made to create widespread irrigation systems, but the water supply throughout the southern half of the province—and therefore the state of the economy—still depends to a large degree on the vagaries of nature.

Climate

As in much of Canada, winters in Saskatchewan are long and cold, whereas summers are quite pleasant but far too short. Saskatchewan's climate is so harsh that it often receives some credit for the province's communal way of life, because friends and neighbors frequently help each other through the boredom and hardship that can accompany the long, cold months.

Three main climate zones, corresponding roughly to the three geographic zones, cross the province. The northern part of Saskatchewan is the coldest and snowiest. January temperatures average about -23 degrees Fahrenheit (-31 degrees Celsius), with an annual snowfall of approximately 50 inches (130 centimeters). Nearly 100 years ago, the small city of Prince Albert recorded the lowest temperature ever in Saskatchewan: -70°F (-57°C). Summer temperatures in the north average about 57°F (14°C).

To the south, the climate becomes more moderate, although the summers remain short. On the plains, the last spring frost usually comes in early June and the first frost of the winter comes in early September, meaning that the growing season, even in this fertile area, is quite short. July temperatures range from a low of 52°F (11°C) to a high of 81°F (27°C). But in Saskatchewan's far south, in the semidesert valleys along the Frenchman and Big Muddy rivers, temperatures often climb into the 90s and 100s F (30s and 40s C).

The History

Although Saskatchewan has been a province within the confederation of Canada only since 1905, its history is as rich and expansive as its fertile plains. From the arrival of the first natives more than 10,000 years ago until today, when some 1 million people live and work in this vital province, Saskatchewan has played a unique and innovative part in Canada's social and economic development.

Before the first white man arrived in the province in the late 17th century, the area now known as Saskatchewan was inhabited by five Indian peoples belonging to three major Native American language families. The Chipewyan, members of the Athabascan linguistic group, lived in the north, where they hunted caribou and elk in the forests and fished from the rivers and streams. Two groups of Algonquian Indians, the Cree and the Blackfoot, hunted buffalo on the plains in the center of the province, and two groups of Sioux Indians, the Assiniboine and the Gros Ventre, inhabited the valleys south and west of the plains region. Although skirmishes between the tribes occurred, the region's plentiful resources allowed for relative peace until the whites introduced competition for land and wealth.

Opposite: Chief Poundmaker of the Cree Indians, photographed with his wife sometime during the 1880s, fought vigorously but in vain to halt white settlement of Native American lands. *Above:* The fur press, weighted with heavy boulders, was used to compress the furs collected by trappers into bales for shipping.

Frederic Remington, a U.S. artist noted for chronicling the American West in paintings and sculptures, drew this sketch of trappers, Indians, and Mounties gathered in a Hudson's Bay Company store.

The first white man to see Saskatchewan was Henry Kelsey, an employee of the powerful British fur-trading corporation called the Hudson's Bay Company. In 1670, King Charles II of Great Britain granted the company a charter to operate in what was then called Prince Rupert's Land, which included present-day northern Quebec and Ontario, most of Saskatchewan, all of Manitoba, and portions of Alberta and the Northwest Territories. In 1690, Kelsey set up a permanent post in what is now Manitoba to explore this huge western region.

This enterprising young man, 20 years old, set out to befriend the Indian population, thereby ensuring the safety of the traders who would be transporting valuable furs from western outposts in Prince Rupert's Land to the company's main office at York Factory, on the shore of Hudson Bay in Manitoba. Kelsey learned the Cree language and adapted himself to Indian ways during two extensive journeys into the valley of the Saskatchewan River during the summers of 1690 and 1691.

The fur trade flourished. But, although Kelsey's explorations confirmed that the area was rich in resources, the only whites who moved into the territory during the next 50 or 60 years were a few fur trappers and traders. In 1741, a French Canadian fur-trading family named La Vérendrye set up posts along the Saskatchewan River in Manitoba. This brought French settlers to the edge of present-day Saskatchewan. At about the same time, another French Canadian, Louis François de la Corne, a commander of the French trading posts, started an agricultural experiment: growing wheat. This was the beginning of what later became Saskatchewan's impressive wheat farms.

Not until 1774 did Saskatchewan have a permanent settlement of whites. Called Cumberland House, this community was built as a fur-trading post by Samuel Hearne of the Hudson's Bay Company on the banks of Cumberland Lake and the Saskatchewan River. During the following years, other such trading posts were established, mostly in the north. In 1783, a rival of the Hudson's Bay Company's, called the North West Company, joined the competition for the fur resources of Prince Rupert's Land, bringing more explorers and entrepreneurs from the east. The two firms merged in 1821 under the name Hudson's Bay Company.

For the next 50 years, permanent settlement of Prince Rupert's Land was steady but slow. Most new arrivals were British or French people from the provinces of Ontario and Quebec in eastern Canada, and almost all of them were involved in the fur trade. In 1870, the Dominion of Canada purchased Prince Rupert's Land from the Hudson's Bay Company. Now officially a Canadian territory, Prince Rupert's Land was renamed the North West Territories, which included present-day Saskatchewan and Manitoba as well as today's Northwest Territories.

Taming the West

The open prairies and abundant natural resources of the North West Territories beckoned to more and more people from eastern Canada, Europe, and the United States. But three things were necessary before large-scale settlement could begin. First, a reliable and efficient railway system had to be built to connect the huge expanse of territory that was emerging as the Canadian nation. Second, the Indians—including the métis, a people of mixed

Also by Frederic Remington, this drawing of a Mountie shows the details of the uniform that became the symbol of law and order on Canada's wild frontier.

Indian and French descent—had to be subjugated and their lands taken by treaty or by force. Third, and related to both of these goals, law and order had to be established in the wild western lands.

Indeed, as more settlers arrived, the Canadian west began to approach the kind of lawlessness and violence that occurred in the Wild West of the United States. An illegal whiskey trade flourished in the North West Territories, tension between Indians and whites frequently erupted into bloodshed, and a criminal element—including American outlaws such as Butch Cassidy and his gang—carried out exploits in the region or used it as a hideout. The principal threat was war between the Indians and the whites. The Canadian government was afraid that if war broke out, the United States would intervene as an excuse to seize control of territory north of its border. To prevent this, Canada's government created a new law enforcement agency to protect Canada's interests in the Territories: the North West Mounted Police (NWMP), commonly known as the Mounties.

Clad in bright red uniforms similar to those of the British army, this now legendary force of 300 men was armed with pistols and sent into the Territories to keep the peace. In 1875, the first NWMP troop arrived in Saskatchewan's Cypress Hills. In command was Superintendent James Walsh, and the post that was built was named after him; in 1878, Fort Walsh became the headquarters of this growing police force.

One of the Mounties' first assignments was to put a stop to the illegal whiskey trade that was rampant throughout the Territories. Because a great deal of the illegal whiskey was being sold or traded to the Indians, the NWMP soon established close relationships with the various tribes. The generally cordial relations between the Indians and the NWMP actually made it easier for the NWMP to persuade the Indians to sign treaties with the Canadian government. These treaties transferred the Indians' land to the whites in exchange for money and other goods and forced the Indians to live on reserved lands. Some 10 major treaties involving Indian lands in Saskatchewan were signed and enforced during the 19th century as the white man staked his claim.

Tension increased as more and more land was taken from the Indians. As time went on, the job of the often reluctant NWMP—many of whom had become friendly with the Indians—became one of intimidation and bloodshed rather than of peaceful negotiation. Matters worsened when the great Canadian Pacific Railway reached across the southern part of the North West Territories in 1882 and 1883. For the first time, large numbers of settlers were coming not to trap beaver and other fur-bearing animals in the empty northlands but to settle in permanent farming communities across the southern plains. The Cree Indians had hunted buffalo on these plains for centuries; now, however, their age-old way of life was threatened. Battles between the Cree and the NWMP escalated, and the Canadian government once again feared that a full-scale war might erupt.

By 1883, the Canadian Pacific Railway had crossed Saskatchewan. These workers laid the track at Maple Creek, on the edge of Cypress Hills.

The Saskatchewan Uprising

The métis were also affected by the arrival of the railroad and its growing number of passengers. Many of these people of mixed French and Indian heritage had originally lived in Manitoba, on land owned by the Hudson's Bay Company. In 1869, when the company prepared to transfer ownership of this property to the Canadian government, the métis feared further encroachment by

Mystic and rebel, the métis leader Louis Riel remains one of the most controversial figures in Canada's history.

white settlers. The métis demanded that the territory they occupied be admitted to Canada as a full-fledged province, not as a territory, and that they be given full citizenship, including the right to vote and to speak French and Native American dialects instead of English in their schools. The few white settlers who had already arrived in Manitoba opposed the idea of citizenship for the métis and took up arms against them. The métis were led by the charismatic Louis Riel, who was born in Manitoba and educated in Montreal. In 1869–70, they captured the important Fort Garry in Winnipeg and then executed an anti-métis laborer named Thomas Scott.

When Ottawa sent a contingent of troops to quell the métis uprising, Riel fled and the revolt collapsed. Although the government promised to give language and political rights as well as land grants to the métis, most of these promises were not kept when the province of Manitoba was established in 1870; the métis were cheated out of most of their land by agents of the Canadian government. Many of them fled westward to the more sparsely populated Saskatchewan district, where they settled in the valley of the Saskatchewan River.

The arrival of the railroad in Saskatchewan in 1883 awakened old fears of white encroachment among the métis, who asked the government in Ottawa to consider their rights. They were told, however, that they had no legal claim to the Saskatchewan lands on which they lived—if they wished to remain, they would have to apply for grants along with other homesteaders. Frustrated and afraid, the métis called upon their former leader, Louis Riel, who had been living in Montana.

In March 1885, Riel arrived in Batoche, a large métis settlement on the South Saskatchewan River. He organized the increasingly dissatisfied métis, and on March 19—the feast day of St. Joseph, who was regarded by the métis as their patron saint—Riel set up a provisional government with himself at the head. When word came that the Mounties were on their way to arrest Riel, the métis cut telegraph lines and took several whites hostage. But the first real battle occurred a week later, at the small settlement of Duck Lake. Police and métis fought there for about

Standing third from left is White Cap, an Indian warrior who was captured by the 12th Battalion of the York Rangers during the North West Rebellion.

half an hour before the police were forced to retreat; the métis had killed 12 of their men.

News of the métis victory caused fear and outrage back in eastern Canada. At the same time, the government in Ottawa learned that the Cree were also preparing to fight white settlement of the Saskatchewan region. Within a matter of days, militia units from Ontario, Quebec, and Nova Scotia boarded trains heading west. One contingent was sent to fight the Cree, another to stop the métis. This rebellion in the west was the closest Canada would ever come to a civil war.

Both the Cree and the métis fought long and hard, and each scored significant victories before succumbing to the overpowering federal army. A band of Cree, led by Chief Big Bear, took the Frog Lake settlement, killing nine men and wounding scores of others, then forced the evacuation of the NWMP post at Fort Pitt. Chief Poundmaker, too, held the white soldiers at bay, trouncing them in a significant battle at Cut Knife Creek.

Meanwhile, at Fish Lake, the métis successfully ambushed the column of troops that had been sent against them. Two weeks later, however, the troops, headed by Major General Frederick Middleton, advanced on the métis stronghold at Batoche. Outnumbered five to one, the métis fought bravely for four days until Riel and his men could hold out no longer and surrendered.

Hearing of Riel's defeat, Chief Poundmaker surrendered. A few weeks later, after fighting the last battle ever fought on Canadian soil, Big Bear and his men laid down their arms. The two Cree chiefs were sent to jail for two years and Riel, after refusing to plead insanity as his lawyer suggested, was hanged as a traitor. Today, Riel is recognized as one of Saskatchewan's most colorful and controversial characters. The Batoche National Historical Site commemorates the events of his life.

The North West Rebellion ended more than a century ago, but its effects are still felt. One important result of the rebellion was the rush to complete construction of the Canadian Pacific Railway (the last spike was driven in British Columbia, on Canada's west coast, in 1885); had it not been for the railroad, troops from Ottawa would never have been able to arrive in the northwest in time to quell the rebellion.

A less positive aftereffect of the North West Rebellion is the lingering resentment between French Canadians—who by and large supported Louis Riel and the métis—and English-speaking Canadians. The métis' call for political and social rights has been echoed in recent years by the demands of many Canadians of French descent who have long felt that their heritage and culture are being overwhelmed by the more numerous and powerful British.

Saskatchewan Comes into Its Own

With efficient transportation in place and the Indian and métis uprisings quelled, settlement of the North West Territories proceeded apace. The slow trickle of settlers turned into a steady stream, especially after the Canadian government joined the Canadian Pacific Railway in a vigorous campaign to encourage emigration by Europeans to Canada. At the same time, more and more homesteaders from the United States, discovering that inexpensive, fertile land was hard to find at home, decided to seek their fortunes in the north.

Soon the Territories were far too large to manage under just one regional government. In 1905, the Canadian government reorganized the region, carving out two new provinces: Saskatchewan and its western neighbor, Alberta. Seven years later, the present-day Northwest Territories officially became part of the Canadian nation.

And the population continued to mount. In 1885, when the Canadian Pacific Railway completed its span across Saskatchewan, the population of the district was slightly more than 32,000. About half of these early citizens were British, and half were Indian. Twenty-five years later, 5 years after Saskatchewan became a province, the population had grown by approximately 1,500 percent. Nearly half a million people—a population of 493,000—called Saskatchewan home in 1911. More than half of these were neither British nor Indian. Germans, Ukrainians, Poles, Czechs, and Scandinavians were flocking to the plains, eager to make their fortunes growing wheat to feed the burgeoning population of North America.

Everywhere in southern and central Saskatchewan, villages and towns were founded by the new settlers. Two cities were especially important to the province's development. Saskatoon, located on the South Saskatchewan River, was founded in 1882 as a temperance colony by a small group of antiliquor zealots from Ontario. Because of its favorable location on the river, however, Saskatoon attracted thousands of new settlers. When Saskatchewan became a province, there was talk of making this booming city—no longer "dry"—the new province's capital.

Unfortunately for Saskatoon, another city with an equally unusual origin won the honor of becoming the capital. Pile O'Bones, so named because of the enormous number of buffalo bones left there by ardent hunters, was a tiny hunting village founded in early pioneer days. When the North West Mounted Police made their headquarters there in 1882, however, Pile O'Bones was renamed Regina (Latin for "queen") after Queen Victoria of Great Britain. Later that year, Regina was designated the capital of the North West Territories. When it came time to select Saskatchewan's provincial capital in 1906, Regina, with a population of approximately 23,000, was the natural choice.

The province's population was growing by leaps and bounds,

During the 1930s, a worldwide economic depression dried up the flow of money into Saskatchewan, and a prolonged drought dried out the soil. Dust and sand drifted across the roads and fields, and many homesteaders left the barren land in despair.

Despite their defeat at the hands of the Royal Canadian Mounted Police in the 1935 Regina Riot, these unemployed workers vowed to proceed "On to Ottawa" to present their grievances to the federal government.

and so was its agricultural production. Wheat prices were soaring. Thousands of farmers across the vast plains began growing this valuable crop by the ton. After World War I broke out in 1914, Saskatchewan was able to provide Great Britain and its allies with substantial supplies of food during the war years.

After the war ended in 1918, however, wheat prices fell and farmers across the province suffered. During this period the province began to assess its status and position within the nation. Many people from Saskatchewan felt that federal policies, formed in the increasingly industrial east, were not always well suited to the needs of a province whose economy was firmly based on farming. In an effort to help strengthen their economic position, the farmers of Saskatchewan created the Saskatchewan Wheat Pool, a cooperative organization that marketed wheat in an orderly and stable manner, selling directly to importers of wheat in other countries. Profits were divided annually among members.

The wheat pool remains one of Saskatchewan's most impressive organizations; it was one of many provincial political and social innovations.

Although agriculture remained the province's main economic activity, mining began to gain importance. Coal was mined in the south, copper and zinc in the north. Efforts to diversify the economy were especially important as the number of people in Saskatchewan continued to increase. In the mid-1930s, however, population growth leveled off at about 950,000, and the province's population has remained close to that mark since then.

The Dirty Thirties

The Great Depression that fell upon the world in 1929 hit Saskatchewan particularly hard. Wheat prices crashed along with the stock market. To make matters worse, a devastating drought that lasted through most of the 1930s crippled the entire grain-producing region of North America. Every year, less rain fell and less wheat grew—at the same time, wheat prices continued to drop, so farmers earned less money than ever for what they did manage to produce. Tens of thousands of farmers were forced to leave their homes; hunger and poverty took the place of the bulging storehouses of wheat of a few years before.

As economic conditions worsened, political agitation increased. The Mounties, now known as the Royal Canadian Mounted Police (RCMP), were frequently called upon to quell violent demonstrations by hungry, angry citizens. In 1931, the RCMP killed three workers during a coal miners' strike in the southern town of Estevan. In 1935, unemployed workers boarded a train in Vancouver in British Columbia, heading for Ottawa to present a list of grievances to the federal government. They were joined by other protesters at stops along the way. But on July 1, the RCMP stopped the train at Regina and forced the protesters, now numbering 2,000, off the train. The violent clash that followed is known as the Regina Riot; scores of both police and protesters were injured.

John Diefenbaker, who became the prime minister of Canada in 1957, was Saskatchewan's best-known political figure.

Throughout Saskatchewan and, indeed, the world, the Great Depression caused many people to reconsider political and economic priorities. Radical ideas flourished and socialism—an economic philosophy that rejected free-market capitalism in favor of cooperation and state ownership of land and industry—began to gain momentum. Saskatchewan was at the forefront of this movement, hosting in Regina the first convention of a new political party, the Co-operative Commonwealth Federation (CCF). The CCF issued the Regina Manifesto, a statement that called for a number of progressive programs: a national labor code, encouragement of cooperatives that workers would own as well as run, and free hospital and medical care for all.

Although the CCF was a national party, it was most popular in Saskatchewan. In fact, Saskatchewan elected the first socialist government in North American history when Tommy Douglas of the CCF became provincial prime minister in 1944. Within months of this election, many of the proposals in the Regina Manifesto were passed into law in the province.

The CCF, which became the New Democratic party (NDP) when it merged with several labor parties in 1961, did much to define modern Saskatchewan. This socialist party governed the province from 1944 to 1964, two decades during which Saskatchewan led the nation in enacting progressive social programs. In 1947, Saskatchewan became the first province to provide free hospital care for its citizens; later this benefit was extended to include most private medical care as well. Saskatchewan's innovative approach was the model for the national health program enacted by Canada's federal government in 1967.

Ironically, however, it was a Conservative party politician who became one of Saskatchewan's most powerful and renowned personalities. John Diefenbaker, born in Grey County, Ontario, came to Saskatchewan at the age of eight. He grew up to be a remarkably popular politician in Saskatchewan and throughout Canada. He served as Canada's 13th prime minister (from 1957 to 1963) and was the first Conservative party leader to be prime minister in more than 20 years. Diefenbaker's charismatic personality and impassioned politics gave Saskatchewan both national and international prominence.

Saskatchewan Today

Contemporary Saskatchewan is as proud of its lively politics as it is of its celebrated plains of wheat. In 1964, the Liberal party defeated the NDP. The Liberals stayed in power for nearly 10 years, and then the NDP took power again. But even when the Conservatives won the election for the first time in provincial history in 1982, Saskatchewan's distinctively progressive, cooperative policies remained largely unchanged. Differences among political parties in Saskatchewan are usually matters of degree, not of political philosophy—for example, parties may disagree about

Viacheslav Fetisov, a Soviet
hockey player who later played
in the National Hockey League,
is greeted by Saskatchewanian
Jeane Sauve, the first woman
to serve as Canada's governor-
general.

what percentage of industry and agriculture should be coopera-
tively managed but not about whether cooperative management is
necessary or about how Saskatchewan can best use its economic
and political clout in federal affairs. During the second half of the
20th century, Saskatchewan has sought to find its economic and
political place in Canada and in the world. Industrialization and
urbanization have come more slowly to Saskatchewan than to
other parts of North America, but in 1990 more than 60 percent
of Saskatchewanians were city or town dwellers. Unfortunately,
modern urban problems such as racial tension, crime, and unem-
ployment are appearing in Saskatchewan's landscape along with
the skyscrapers that have sprung up in Saskatoon and Regina.
But the province's unique pioneer spirit, with its abiding qualities
of cooperation and friendship, remains strong, and Saskatchewan
faces the 21st century with enthusiasm, its innovative politics still
inspiring the nation.

The Economy

For almost two centuries after the first white homesteaders arrived on Saskatchewan's soil in the late 18th century, agriculture was the region's largest source of income. Although farming has been outranked by the service industries and is now the second most productive economic activity, it remains vitally important to the province and the country. Saskatchewan is by far the biggest wheat producer in Canada and one of the largest in the world. In 1986, the province grew nearly 13 million tons of wheat (about half of that produced by all other Canadian provinces combined).

Saskatchewan contains about 65 million acres (26 million hectares) of farmland—more than any other province and about 40 percent of Canada's total farmland. It has approximately 60,000 farms. Wheat is grown on most of them, but other grain crops are also important. One of the most successful of the specialty crops is rapeseed, introduced to Saskatchewan during World War II; nearly 50 years later it is the province's third most valuable crop, after wheat and barley. Oil from the seed is refined in Saskatchewan and used in margarine, salad oils, and other products. The province produces nearly 50 percent of all of Canada's rapeseed. About 45 percent of the country's flax, a

Opposite: At an open-pit coal mine near Estevan, an equipment operator controls a huge shovel. Mining is an important contributor to the province's economy.

Above: Saskatchewan has about 3 million head of cattle. Some are dairy cows, such as these on a farm near the town of Rosthern, south of Prince Albert. Others are beef cattle that graze in Cypress Hills.

A harvesting combine, shrouded in a haze of dust and chaff, churns across a wheat field. Approximately 40 percent of Canada's farmland is found in Saskatchewan.

plant from which textiles are made, is also produced in Saskatchewan. Hardy grains are the principal crops, but in certain regions, such as the Qu'Appelle River Valley just north of Regina, potatoes and other vegetables are grown to be sent to market in Regina and Saskatoon. Saskatchewan's unpredictable rainfall and the thin soil in many regions make it difficult to cultivate other food crops.

In addition to cash crops, Saskatchewan also invests in cattle ranching and hog and poultry raising. The province has about 3 million head of cattle. Cypress Hills in the southwestern part of the province is Saskatchewan's best-known ranching country. The lush grass attracted ranchers to the area as early as 1885.

Like all modern agricultural economies, Saskatchewan's is marked by a decrease in the number of small farms. The province has the lowest proportion of small and moderate-sized farms in Canada. As large-scale, more efficient farming methods are introduced, people look outside the agricultural economy for employment.

Since the 1950s, the development of mining in Saskatchewan has been almost as spectacular as that of agriculture. By the late 1980s, mining ranked third, after service industries and agriculture, as a contributor to the province's income. The three most important mineral products are oil, potash, and uranium.

Saskatchewan produces about 10 to 15 percent of Canada's crude oil, with wells pumping a total of nearly 70 million barrels of petroleum a year. Potash mining has also developed rapidly and is Saskatchewan's second-ranking mining industry, accounting for approximately 30 percent of mineral production in the 1980s. Since 1950, when uranium was discovered in the Lake Athabasca region, about half of Canada's uranium has been mined in Saskatchewan.

Agriculture and mining are extremely important to Saskatchewan's economy, but the service industries have become preeminent. Sixty-five percent of the provincial gross domestic product is accounted for by these industries, which include education and health care, advertising and publishing, restaurants and retail stores, transportation and utilities, banking, finance, and insurance.

Both farming and mining require a great deal of capital— that is, money to invest in land, equipment, and workers—and Saskatchewan has always relied upon investment from federal and foreign sources outside the province. There are 400 branches of chartered banks in the province, and there are also some 275 credit unions, in which each depositor is part owner of the corporation. More than half of all Saskatchewanian adults belong to a credit union. The cooperative spirit that pervades agriculture and is best represented by the wheat pool also occurs in virtually every segment of Saskatchewan's economy, including the retailing and distributing trades.

Saskatchewan hopes to increase its manufacturing output. The rapid industrialization that occurred throughout much of

Canada during the early part of the 20th century never reached Saskatchewan, which ranks just eighth or ninth out of the 12 provinces in the value of its manufactured goods. Industry has lagged both because of the province's relatively small population and because agriculture has dominated its economic history. Government policies have also hindered efforts to create an industrial base. For example, the government has placed high tariffs, or import taxes, on materials such as farm equipment shipped into Canada from the United States and other nations. It is therefore cheaper for a farmer in western Canada to buy a tractor made in eastern Canada than one made right across the border in the United States, so the result of this policy has been to strengthen industry in eastern Canada. Furthermore, high freight costs make it expensive to ship raw materials into the west and finished goods out. In the late 1980s, there were fewer than 1,000 manu-

Adolph Buchta stands outside his store in Frenchman Butte. Old-fashioned general stores still meet the needs of shoppers in rural communities, but Saskatchewan has its share of shopping centers and supermarkets as well.

facturing establishments in Saskatchewan, and most of them employed fewer than 100 people.

Food processing is the province's chief manufacturing activity. Many cities, including Regina and Saskatoon, have slaughterhouses and meat-packing plants. Saskatoon has a flour mill. Dairy product centers include Moose Jaw, Prince Albert, Regina, Saskatoon, and Yorkton. Other important industries include printing and the production of stone, clay, and glass products.

In the coming years, Saskatchewan plans to diversify its economy. The number of jobs in the service industries, manufacturing, and mining will probably increase. The province may also try to increase its income from several largely untapped resources, including timber, fishing, and tourism. And like most countries, states, and provinces, Saskatchewan will be trying to protect the environment from further damage. This province has been spared many of the major environmental problems that accompany industrialization and urbanization, but the use of synthetic fertilizers and pesticides—many of which find their way into water supplies—is a controversial issue in Saskatchewan and is likely to remain so for some time.

Visiting bird-watchers are taken on a tour of Redberry Lake. Wildlife enthusiasts and sportspeople are increasingly attracted to the province, and Saskatchewanians hope that tourism will play a growing part in their economy. They realize, however, that cautious development and environmental protection are needed to preserve their natural resources.

The People

In 1986, when Canada's last national census was conducted, the province of Saskatchewan had a little more than 1 million people. Although the population appears to be declining somewhat as family farms fall upon hard times and people leave to earn their livelihood elsewhere, Saskatchewan still has one of the most varied populations in the country; it is the only province where people of British and French origin are outnumbered by people from other ethnic groups.

At the beginning of Saskatchewan's history as a Canadian province, the French slightly outnumbered the British—and the Native American population far outnumbered them both. Slowly but steadily, however, the province's unique ethnic mosaic was created. Those who can trace their lineage to Great Britain account for only about 40 percent of the population, the French make up less than 6 percent, and Native Americans account for less than 4 percent of the total population. Other significant groups include the Germans and Austrians (20 percent), the Ukrainians (10 percent), and the Scandinavians (7 percent).

Opposite: A Native American whirls in a traditional dance during the Standing Buffalo Indian Pow-wow, a festival held every summer at a reserve near Fort Qu'Apelle in the southeast.
Above: The Ukrainian influence is seen throughout Saskatchewan, as in the Church of Saints Peter and Paul in the community of Insinger.

Indian beadwork is displayed at the Duck Lake Museum. This and similar crafts are funded as fine arts by the province's innovative Arts Board.

Throughout the province, ethnic enclaves, each with its own culture and traditions, give towns and villages distinctive qualities. The Ukrainians have been particularly successful in preserving their heritage. After the British and the Germans, they are the third largest ethnic group in Saskatchewan. Most of them are descendants of about 100,000 settlers who came to Canada from the steppes of southeastern Russia in the late 19th and early 20th centuries and thrived in the New World as wheat farmers. During festivals and on holidays, Ukrainians celebrate their heritage by dressing in traditional clothing, playing Ukrainian music, and dancing ethnic steps. Also, Germans, Scandinavians, and people from other origins honor their past in traditional ways.

More than 30 Indian reserves are scattered across the province. Many Native Americans still live on these tribal lands, but many others have entered the mainstream of the province's life in the cities and towns.

More than 60 percent of Saskatchewanians live in urban rather than rural settings. Although more people every year move to its growing cities, Saskatchewan is still one of Canada's most rural provinces; in Ontario, by contrast, more than 90 percent of the people are city dwellers.

Education and the Arts

Education is a top priority in Saskatchewan, accounting for a large percentage of government spending. The school system includes some 1,000 schools and 2 major universities—the University of Regina and the University of Saskatchewan in Saskatoon—that educate more than 210,000 men, women, and children. Some of the schools are called "separate" schools—religious schools connected with either Roman Catholic or Protestant denominations. Both public and separate schools are supported by tax dollars collected by the provincial government, but separate schools are administered by private school boards.

The cultural environment also includes about 275 public libraries and many museums. The Saskatchewan Museum of Natural History in Regina, one of the oldest in the province, features

exhibits of native animals and plants, local archaeology, and geology. The Western Development Museum celebrates Saskatchewan's history with four branches, each in a different city and exploring a different theme in the province's development. Saskatchewan has done a great deal to commemorate its past. More than 100 historic markers, many located on the trails used by early hunters, trappers, and the renowned Mounties, identify battlefields, Indian villages, and forts throughout the province.

Largely because of the Saskatchewan Arts Board, created in 1949 by the CCF party, the province does more than revel in its history; contemporary arts thrive in modern Saskatchewan. The first publicly funded council of the arts in North America, the board has done much to stimulate the arts in Saskatchewan. There are professional theater companies, symphony orchestras, dance companies, and museums and art galleries in all of Saskatchewan's major cities.

Modern sculpture has an outdoor setting at the Mendel Art Gallery in Saskatoon. Across the river are the buildings of the University of Saskatchewan.

One of the most important early steps taken by the arts board was to give crafts—such as leather work, silversmithing, and pottery—the status of art so that the province's many craftspeople could benefit from financial support and encouragement along with its painters and performing artists. In recent years there has been a renewed interest in Native American arts and crafts as well as a growing appreciation of the Indians' contribution to Saskatchewan's history and culture.

Pottery is one of Saskatchewan's special treasures. The clayey soil from which sprang the province's great fortunes in wheat also provides artisans with excellent material. Saskatchewan's fine ceramics are known throughout the world.

Sports and Leisure Time

The arts are not the only diversions in Saskatchewan. Amateur and professional sports of all types—from swimming to golf to football—attract hundreds of thousands of participants and fans.

Saskatchewanians are very proud of the province's professional football team, the Roughriders. Founded in 1910 as the Regina Riders, this enthusiastic organization is known as "the

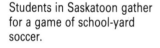

Students in Saskatoon gather for a game of school-yard soccer.

Rodeos are popular, especially in the ranching country of the southwest.

winningest team in the west." In the first 21 years that western championships were held, the Riders won 15 times, starting in 1912. Since then, they have provided stiff competition for teams inside and outside the western league, frequently competing for the national championship of the Canadian Football League—the Grey Cup—and winning it in 1966.

But professional sports satisfy just a portion of the average Saskatchewanian's competitive spirit; amateur sports for both fans and athletes abound. At the high school level, track and field and basketball are the biggest crowd pleasers. The western rodeo, complete with broncobusting and hog-tying, remains one of the best-loved pastimes in the province.

The people of Saskatchewan particularly enjoy outdoor activities: fishing, canoeing, hiking, and skiing, among many others, are extremely popular. Saskatchewan has 24 national and provincial parks for hiking and camping. More than 50 canoe routes offer some of the best canoeing in all of Canada: some of these routes are the original paths taken by the fur traders and French *voyageurs* (explorers) in the 17th and 18th centuries. Walleye, lake trout, and northern pike abound in the province's rivers and lakes. Most of the best fishing is in the north, but the lakes of southern Saskatchewan also attract fishermen from all over Canada.

The Cities

Regina: The Prairie Capital

At first, Regina was not much more than its original name suggested: Pile O'Bones was just a tiny hunting village on the edge of Wascana Creek. Today, however, it deserves its regal name. An oasis of trees and water in the midst of seemingly endless prairie, Regina is a thriving capital city of more than 175,000 people.

The provincial government is by far the largest employer in Regina, but other major corporations and organizations are also located here. The Saskatchewan Wheat Pool, for instance, employs about 4,000 people and has annual sales in excess of $2 billion. The service industries, including health care, education, advertising, and tourism, are the strongest economic presence in the city.

As the agricultural market remains as unpredictable as ever, Regina is diversifying its economy. In recent decades, the city has added the largest steel mill in western Canada, many oil refineries, and a number of manufacturers, especially food producers, to its economic base.

Opposite: The province's legislature meets in this building, surrounded by flowers in Regina's downtown Wascana Center.
Above: Called the City of Bridges, Saskatoon straddles the South Saskatchewan River. The population of Saskatoon is slightly larger than that of Regina, the capital of the province.

Regina's economic growth is impressive, but its physical beauty is unmatched in the region. The people of the city have worked hard to make it the beautiful provincial centerpiece it is today. The heart of the city is Wascana Center, a 2,500-acre (1,000-hectare) park in which the legislative buildings are located. Wascana Center is full of things to see and do, including the Saskatchewan Center of the Arts, the Museum of Natural History, and the University of Regina, but perhaps its most popular attraction is Wascana Lake.

This man-made body of water, formed by the damming of Wascana Creek in 1905 and later deepened and widened during the 1930s, is a magnet for both city residents and tourists alike. They swim in the lake and boat on it or have picnics and barbecues on its shores, thus enjoying the great outdoors right downtown in the capital.

Another landmark in Regina, also tied to its early history, is the Royal Canadian Mounted Police barracks. RCMP recruits from all over Canada receive special training in criminal investigation and other techniques in the Regina branch, which also has an excellent museum tracing the RCMP's illustrious history.

Saskatoon: The City of Bridges

In the late 1980s, Saskatoon, long known as Saskatchewan's Second City, surpassed its competitor, Regina, in population. More than 177,000 people call Saskatoon home, thriving in the major trading center of western Canada.

Sometimes called the Hub City, Saskatoon is served by all the major highways and railroads of the region. It is the central marketplace for a farming area of about 70,000 square miles (180,000 square kilometers). The University of Saskatchewan, founded here in 1911, is the city's largest employer, followed closely by the city government. Food production, especially meat packing and dairying, are mainstays of the city's industrial economy.

Geographically, Saskatoon marks the end of the prairie and the beginning of Saskatchewan's northern parkland. This location

provides easy access to the province's many valuable mineral deposits. During the 1960s, Saskatoon became one of the largest supply centers for the province's mining industry; by the late 1980s, factories that manufactured equipment and processed the ores employed thousands of Saskatoon's workers. Potash mining supports a significant sector of the local economy.

Saskatoon covers about 53 square miles (138 square kilometers) on both sides of the South Saskatchewan River. It is called the City of Bridges because seven bridges connect the two banks of the river. Most of the heavy industry is located at the edge of the city, and tree-lined streets and wide avenues give Saskatoon an air of elegance rivaling that of the capital.

Frenchman Butte, on the North Saskatchewan River, is typical of the province's many small towns. It was a fur-trading post from 1829 to 1890.

Moose Jaw, west of Regina, is a modern industrial city. During the 1920s it was a wild, rough-edged town, where U.S. gangster Al Capone is said to have hidden from the law.

In addition to its physical beauty, Saskatoon offers a host of cultural attractions. The University of Saskatchewan, Kelsey University, and the Cooperative College of Canada are the city's major educational institutions, attracting scholars from all over Canada. Saskatoon is also the center of Ukrainian culture and history. The Ukrainian Museum of Canada and the Yevshan Ukrainian Folk-Ballet Company are located there.

Situated on the west bank of the South Saskatchewan, the Mendel Art Gallery and Civic Conservatory boasts one of the most extensive collections of works by famous Canadian painters as well as an excellent collection of historical and contemporary Saskatchewanian art. It also hosts many traveling international exhibits. Like Regina, Saskatoon has an active theater scene, its own symphony orchestra, and a superb concert hall. Every summer, the "Shakespeare on the Saskatchewan" festival features a different Shakespearean play.

Prince Albert: Gateway to the North

Located on the banks of the North Saskatchewan River, Prince Albert, known as the Gateway to the North, has a population of about 34,000. Named for Queen Victoria's husband, Prince Albert was founded in 1866 as a Presbyterian mission. The town grew rapidly at first as the fur trade expanded, but the boom collapsed when the Canadian Pacific Railway chose a more southern route. In 1990 only 2 percent of Saskatchewan's 1 million citizens made their homes in the rugged north; most of these are métis or Blackfoot Indians.

In an attempt to bring prosperity back to the area, the city tried to build a hydroelectric power plant during the late 1880s at La Colle Falls, hoping that inexpensive electricity would attract industry. These dreams were never realized, however, and the project brought Prince Albert to the verge of bankruptcy. For decades, the city's economy was depressed and stagnant, until efforts were made to develop its major resources: logging, fishing, and, with its abundant wildlife and beautiful landscape, tourism.

One of the area's greatest attractions is Prince Albert National Park, established in 1927. Located about 200 miles (320 kilometers) north of Saskatoon and covering about 1,479 square miles (3,874 square kilometers), this magnificent park contains boreal forests, prairie grasslands, and dozens of lakes. The park is rich in wildlife—elks, moose, and deer are found in the aspen forests, while wolves and caribou roam the forests of jack pine, larch, and balsam fir. More than 195 species of birds have been spotted in this rich and varied landscape.

A totem pole on a riverbank in Prince Albert National Park is just one of many signs of the high concentration of Indians and métis in the northern part of the province.

Things to Do and See

• **Royal Canadian Mounted Police Museum,** Regina: Documents the history of the force from its beginnings to the present day. Contains uniforms, weapons, flags, documents, and other artifacts relating to the heritage of the Mounties.

• **Wascana Center,** Regina: 2,500 acres (1,000 hectares) of parkland and important buildings, including the provincial legislature, museums, the art center, and the University of Regina. Also has picnic areas and swimming and boating facilities.

• **Museum of Natural History,** Regina: Displays Saskatchewan's wildlife and archeological wonders in dioramas and other exhibits.

• **Saskatchewan Center of the Arts,** Regina: Hosts performances by major provincial, national, and international orchestras and theater, opera, and dance companies. Home of the Regina Symphony Orchestra.

Opposite: Dressed in a moosehide jacket, a competitor in the King Trapper contest bakes old-fashioned bannock bread at the Prince Albert Winter Festival.
Above: The Snowbirds are Canada's premier stunt-flying team. Their home is the Canadian Air Force Base on the outskirts of Moose Jaw, which has become Canada's busiest airport because of the air force traffic.

• **Mendel Art Gallery,** Saskatoon: One of western Canada's most important public galleries, featuring paintings by Chagall, Pissarro, and other artists of international and provincial repute.

• **Western Development Museum,** Yorkton, Moose Jaw, Saskatoon, Battleford: Various chapters of Saskatchewan's history told at four different branches of this unique museum. At Yorkton, social history is explored; at Moose Jaw, the story of transportation is told; Saskatoon re-creates the Canadian west around 1910 in its Boomtown Saskatchewan, a street of stores and homes created to match turn-of-the-century Saskatchewan; at Battleford, a living historical farm grows and harvests its crops using methods and machinery of the early 20th century.

• **Wanuskewin Heritage Park,** Saskatoon: A celebration of Native American life and culture, featuring 8,000-year-old artifacts and rock paintings, tours, and walking trails. Scheduled to open to the public in 1992.

• **Ukrainian Museum of Canada,** Saskatoon: Explores the unique contribution to the province by Ukrainians with displays of crafts, weavings, costumes, and other historical artifacts.

• **Diefenbaker Homestead,** Wascana Center, Regina: Displays memorabilia from the life of John Diefenbaker, Canada's 13th prime minister and one of Saskatchewan's most prominent citizens.

• **Canadian Air Force Base,** Moose Jaw: Home of Canada's most famous team of high-flying stunt pilots, the Snowbirds.

• **Wood Mountain Historic Park,** Wood Mountain Village: The site of the first NWMP depots, with historical artifacts and memorabilia.

• **Sports Hall of Fame,** Regina: Honors athletes from all over Saskatchewan, including hockey legend Gordie Howe and football star Ron Lancaster.

Megamunch, a moving, roaring model of a *Tyrannosaurus rex,* is one of the attractions of Regina's Museum of Natural History.

The interior of the Ukrainian Church of Saints Peter and Paul in Canora features magnificent religious paintings and elaborate ornamentation.

• **Hudson's Bay Company Museum,** Fort Qu'Appelle: Displays Indian artifacts as well as objects from the early history of this famous fur-trading company. Adjoins an original 1864 Hudson's Bay Company post.

• **Centennial Museum,** Earl Grey: Features old machines, pioneer artifacts, and turn-of-the-century books and catalogs.

• **Moose Jaw Wild Animal Park,** Moose Jaw: Three hundred acres containing buffalo, elks, yaks, and deer. Also features lions, leopards, and other exotic mammals and has a children's petting zoo.

Skaters glide over the frozen South Saskatchewan River during a Saskatoon winter. The Bessborough Hotel is in the background.

Festivals & Holidays

Winter: Towns and villages all over Saskatchewan host **Winter Carnivals** featuring ice skating, snowmobile races, skiing, and log-sawing and wood-chopping competitions. February finds Estevan holding the **International 250 Snowmobile Race** from Regina to Minot. Prince Albert hosts the **Championship Dog Derby,** in which 8 dogsled teams compete in a 3-day, 48-mile (77-kilometer) race.

Spring: In April, Weyburn has a **Pee-Wee Hockey Tournament** and Lloydminster is the site of a huge **Carnival.** In May, the **International Marching Bands Competition** is held in Regina, the **Cross-country Hang Gliding Classic** takes place in the Qu'Appelle Valley, and a major film festival, **The Golden Sheaf Awards,** is held in Yorkton.

Summer: Saskatchewan really comes alive during the summer months. June finds a **Model Airplane Show** in Moose Jaw and the **Kinsman Rodeo Western Days** in Unity. Regina is particularly busy, with the **International Kite Festival;** a multicultural ethnic celebration called **Mosaic;** and the **Western Canada Farm**

Progress Show. Also in June, North Battleford displays pioneer machinery and tools in a reconstructed pioneer village, complete with a parade and harness racing. **The Trial of Louis Riel,** a dramatic reenactment of the trial of the charismatic métis leader, takes place in July and August in Regina. Saskatoon hosts the **Shakespeare on the Saskatchewan Festival** and one of the province's largest exhibitions of farm machinery and livestock, the **Saskatoon Exhibition.** In mid-July, Moose Jaw is the site of one of the largest air shows in North America, the **Saskatchewan Air Show.** Indian culture and heritage can be experienced at the **Chief Poundmaker Memorial Pow-Wow** in Cut Knife in July and at the **Standing Buffalo Indian Pow-Wow** at Fort Qu'Appelle in early August. At the end of August, Regina hosts 10 days of pioneer celebration, including horse racing, rodeos, fairs, and band concerts during its **Buffalo Days Exhibition.**

Fall: Swift Current holds its annual **Harvest Festival** in September, right before it hosts the **Western Canadian Olde Tyme Fiddling Contest.** For chili lovers, Saskatoon has the **Saskatchewan Open Chili Cookoff** in mid-September. In October, the large German population of St. Walburg and other towns in Saskatchewan hold **Oktoberfests,** complete with parades and entertainment. In late November, Regina holds its annual **Mexabition and Agribition,** an international livestock and farm machinery show.

A carnival midway, complete with fairground rides, was one of the attractions of the 1987 Saskatoon Exhibition.

Chronology

1670	King Charles II of Great Britain grants trading rights in the Saskatchewan region to the Hudson's Bay Company.
1690–92	Henry Kelsey of the Hudson's Bay Company explores along the Saskatchewan River.
1740s	The La Vérendrye family of French Canadian fur traders build trading posts on the Saskatchewan River.
1774	Hudson's Bay Company establishes Cumberland House, Saskatchewan's first permanent white settlement.
1870	Canada acquires Prince Rupert's Land from the Hudson's Bay Company and calls it the North West Territories.
1882–83	The Canadian Pacific Railway is built across the Saskatchewan region.
1885	The métis rebel against the Canadian government.
1905	Saskatchewan becomes a Canadian province on September 1.
1924	Farmers organize the Saskatchewan Wheat Pool.
1944	The voters of Saskatchewan elect the first socialist government in Canada.
1951	Petroleum is discovered in Saskatchewan.
1964	The Liberal party defeats the socialists.
1982	The Progressive Conservative party wins provincial elections.
1986	Expo '86 is held in Saskatchewan.
1989	The 1989 Jeux Canada Games (the "Canadian Olympics") are held in Saskatoon.

Further Reading

Berton, Pierre. *The Impossible Railway: The Building of the Canadian Pacific.* Magnolia, Manitoba: Peter Smith, 1984.

Breen, David H. *The Canadian Prairie West and the Ranching Frontier.* Toronto: University of Toronto Press, 1983.

Ewars, John C. *The Blackfeet: Raiders on the Northwestern Plains.* Norman: University of Oklahoma Press, 1985.

Holbrook, Sabra. *Canada's Kids.* New York: Atheneum, 1983.

Howard, James H. *The Canadian Sioux.* Lincoln: University of Nebraska Press, 1984.

Kurelek, William. *A Prairie Boy's Summer.* Boston: Houghton Mifflin, 1975.

Law, Kevin. *Canada.* New York: Chelsea House, 1990.

Lipset, Seymour M. *American Socialism: The Cooperative Commonwealth Federation in Saskatchewan: A Study in Political Sociology.* Berkeley: University of California Press, 1971.

MacLeod, R. C., ed. *Reminiscences of a Bungle and Two Other Northwest Rebellion Diaries.* Lincoln: University of Nebraska Press, 1983.

McNaught, Kenneth. *The Penguin History of Canada.* New York: Penguin, 1988.

Malcolm, Andrew. *The Canadians.* New York: Random House, 1985.

Newman, Peter C. *Caesars of the Wilderness: The Story of the Hudson's Bay Company.* New York: Penguin, 1988.

Shephard, Jennifer. *Enchantment of the World: Canada.* Chicago: Childrens Press, 1987.

Sprague, D. N. *Canada and the Métis: 1869–1885.* Atlantic Highlands, New Jersey: Humanities, 1988.

Walsh, Frederick G. *The Trial of Louis Riel.* Fargo: North Dakota Institute for Regional Studies, 1965.

Wansborough, M. B. *Great Canadian Lives.* New York: Doubleday, 1986.

Index

A
Alberta, 9, 14
Assiniboine, 19
Athabasca, Lake, 13–14

B
Batoche, 25, 26
Batoche National Historical
    Site, 27
Big Bear, 26–27
Big Muddy Badlands, 13
Big Muddy River, 17
Blackfoot Indians, 19, 53

C
Canadian Football League, 47
Canadian Pacific Railway, 23,
    27, 28, 53
Canadian Shield, 10
Cassidy, Butch, 22
Charles II, king of England, 20
Chipewyan Indians, 19
Churchill River, 13
Conservative party, 33
Cooperative College of
    Canada, 52
Co-operative Commonwealth
    Federation (CCF), 32, 33,
    45
Cree Indians, 14, 19, 23, 26
Cumberland House, 21
Cut Knife Creek, 26
Cypress Hills, 13, 22, 38

D
Diefenbaker, John, 33
Diefenbaker, Lake, 15
Douglas, Tommy, 32
Duck Lake, 25

E
Estevan, 31

F
Fish Lake, 26
Fort Garry, 25

Fort Pitt, 26
Fort Walsh, 22
François de la Corne, Louis, 21
Free-market capitalism, 32
Frenchman River, 17

G
Great Britain, 30, 43
Great Depression, 31–32
Great Sand Hills, 13
Grey County, 33
Grey Cup, 47
Gros Ventre Indians, 19

H
Hearne, Samuel, 21
Hudson Bay, 20
Hudson's Bay Company, 20–
    21, 23

K
Kelsey, Henry, 20
Kelsey University, 52
Kisiskadjewan, 14

L
La Colle Falls, 53
La Vérendrye, 21

M
Mackenzie River, 13
Manitoba, 9, 14, 20, 21, 25
Mendel Art Gallery and Civic
    Conservatory, 52
Métis, 19, 21–25
Middleton, Frederick, 26
Montana, 25
Montreal, 25
Moose Jaw, 41
Mounties, 25, 31, 45. *See also*
    North West Mounted
    Police; Royal Canadian
    Mounted Police
Mun-a-tuk-gaw, 13

N
New Democratic party
    (NDP), 33

North Saskatchewan River, 14
North West Company, 21
North West Mounted Police
    (NWMP), 22–23, 26, 28
North West Rebellion, 27
North West Territories, 21,
    22, 23, 27, 28
Northwest Territories, 9, 20,
    21, 28
Nova Scotia, 26

O
Ontario, 20, 21, 26, 28, 44
Ottawa, 25, 26, 27, 31

P
Pile O' Bones, 28, 49
Poundmaker, 26–27
Prince Albert, 10, 17, 41, 53
Prince Albert National Park, 53
Prince Rupert's Land, 20, 21.
    See also North West Terri-
    tories

Q
Qu'Appelle-Assiniboine River,
    13
Qu'Appelle River Valley, 38
Quebec, 20, 21, 26

R
Regina, 28, 31–32, 35, 38,
    41, 44, 49, 52
Regina, University of, 44, 50
Regina Manifesto, 32, 33
Regina Riot, 31
Riel, Louis, 25, 27
Rocky Mountains, 15
Royal Canadian Mounted
    Police (RCMP), 31, 50
Russia, 44

S
Saskatchewan
    area, 9
    central region, 11–13

climate, 17
early settlement, 20–22
economy, 37–41
education and arts, 44–46
mining, 10–11, 39
natural resources, 10–11
physical features, 9
politics, 30–35
population, 43
and socialism, 32–33
Ukrainian influence, 44
urbanization, 35
waterways, 13–25
wheat production, 9, 21, 37
Saskatchewan, University of, 44, 50, 52
Saskatchewan Arts Board, 45
Saskatchewan Center of the Arts, 50

Saskatchewan Museum of Natural History, 44–45, 50
Saskatchewan River, 13, 14, 21, 25
Saskatchewan Roughriders, 46
Saskatchewan Wheat Pool, 49
Saskatoon, 28, 35, 41, 44, 50–53
Scott, Thomas, 25
Sioux Indians, 19
Socialism, 32–33
South Saskatchewan River, 14, 16, 25, 38

U
Ukrainian Museum of Canada, 52
United States, 9, 21, 22, 27
Uranium City, 14

V
Vancouver, 31
Victoria, queen of England, 28, 53

W
Walsh, James, 22
Wascana Center, 50
Wascana Creek, 50
Wascana Lake, 50
Western Development Museum, 45
Winnipeg, Lake, 14
World War I, 30
World War II, 37

Y
Yevshan Ukrainian Folk-Ballet Company, 52
Yorkton, 41

ACKNOWLEDGMENTS

The Bettmann Archive: pp. 20, 21; Diana Blume: p. 6; Courtesy Canadian Consulate: pp. 8, 9, 10, 12, 14, 16, 47; Courtesy City of Moose Jaw: pp. 52, 55; Karpan photo: cover, pp. 3, 5, 11, 15, 36, 37, 38, 40, 41, 42, 43, 44, 45, 46, 48, 49, 51, 53, 54, 56, 57, 58, 59; Reuters/Bettmann Archive: p. 34; Saskatchewan Archives Board: pp. 18, 19, 23, 24, 26, 29, 30, 32; Debora Smith: p. 7

Suzanne LeVert has contributed several volumes to Chelsea House's LET'S DISCOVER CANADA series. She is the author of four previous books for young readers. One of these, *The Sakharov File*, biography of noted Russian physicist Andrei Sakharov, was selected as a Notable Book by the National Council for the Social Studies. Her other books include *AIDS: In Search of a Killer*, *The Doubleday Book of Famous Americans*, and *New York*. Ms. LeVert also has extensive experience as an editor, first in children's books at Simon & Schuster, then as associate editor at *Trialogue*, the magazine of the Trilateral Commission, and as senior editor at Save the Children, the international relief and development organization. She lives in Cambridge, Massachusetts.

George Sheppard, General Editor, is a lecturer on Canadian and American history at McMaster University in Hamilton, Ontario. Dr. Sheppard holds an honors B.A. and an M.A. in history from Laurentian University and earned his Ph.D. in Canadian history at McMaster. He has taught Canadian history at Nipissing University in North Bay. His research specialty is the War of 1812, and he has published articles in *Histoire sociale/Social History*, *Papers of the Bibliographical Society of Canada*, and *Ontario History*. Dr. Sheppard is a native of Timmins, Ontario.

Pierre Berton, Senior Consulting Editor, is the author of 34 books, including *The Mysterious North*, *Klondike*, *Great Canadians*, *The Last Spike*, *The Great Railway Illustrated*, *Hollywood's Canada*, *My Country: The Remarkable Past*, *The Wild Frontier*, *The Invasion of Canada*, *Why We Act Like Canadians*, *The Klondike Quest*, and *The Arctic Grail*. He has won three Governor General's Awards for creative nonfiction, two National Newspaper Awards, and two ACTRA "Nellies" for broadcasting. He is a Companion of the Order of Canada, a member of the Canadian News Hall of Fame, and holds 12 honorary degrees. Raised in the Yukon, Mr. Berton began his newspaper career in Vancouver. He then became managing editor of *McLean's*, Canada's largest magazine, and subsequently worked for the Canadian Broadcasting Network and the *Toronto Star*. He lives in Kleinburg, Ontario.